PUFFIN BOOKS

# THE DAY THE SMELLS WENT WRONG

Catherine Sefton is the pen-name of Martin Waddell. He has written many books for children of all ages. He has won a number of awards including the Smarties Prize, the Kurt Maschler Award, the Other Award, and was a runner-up for the *Guardian* Children's Fiction Award. He now lives by the sea in Northern Ireland with his wife, three sons and their dog, Bessie

# Catherine Sefton
# The Day the Smells Went Wrong

Illustrated by John Rogan

PUFFIN BOOKS

PUFFIN BOOKS

Published by the Penguin Group
Penguin Books Ltd, 80 Strand, London WC2R 0RL, England
Penguin Putnam Inc., 375 Hudson Street, New York, New York 10014, USA
Penguin Books Australia Ltd, 250 Camberwell Road, Camberwell, Victoria 3124, Australia
Penguin Books Canada Ltd, 10 Alcorn Avenue, Toronto, Ontario, Canada M4V 3B2
Penguin Books India (P) Ltd, 11 Community Centre, Panchsheel Park, New Delhi – 110 017, India
Penguin Books (NZ) Ltd, Cnr Rosedale and Airborne Roads, Albany, Auckland, New Zealand
Penguin Books (South Africa) (Pty) Ltd, 24 Sturdee Avenue, Rosebank 2196, South Africa

Penguin Books Ltd, Registered Offices: 80 Strand, London WC2R 0RL, England

www.penguin.com

First published by Hamish Hamilton Ltd 1988
Published in Puffin Books 1995
Published in this edition 2001
3 5 7 9 10 8 6 4 2

Text copyright © Catherine Sefton, 1988
Illustrations copyright © John Rogan, 1988
All rights reserved

Set in  M Times New Roman School Book

Printed in Hong Kong by Midas Printing Ltd

British Library Cataloguing in Publication Data
A CIP catalogue record for this book is available from the British Library

ISBN 0–141–31300–5

Jackie and Phil had buttered toast
for breakfast.

"Mum?" said Phil. "This toast
smells of tar."

"Just eat it!" said Mum, who was
flying round collecting baby bits
and pushchairs and had no time to
talk.

"We don't want to," said Jackie
and Phil.

Mum was annoyed, but she hadn't
time to fight about it.

1

"All right," she said. "Leave it."

They piled out of the house in a scurry of schoolbags and pushchairs, and then they had to single file down the pavement outside, where the men were putting fresh tar on the road.

*Sniff* went Jackie.

*Sniff-sniff* went Phil.

"That tar smells of toast!" said
Phil.

"And our toast smells of tar!" said
Jackie.

"Oh!" said Somebody.

"Did you say 'Oh'?" said Phil to
Jackie.

"No, you did!" said Jackie.

They went past the Fruit Shop.

*Sniff* went Jackie.

*Sniff-sniff* went Phil.

"Mum, that fruit shop smells of fi ..." began Jackie, but Mum grabbed her arm. They hustled around the corner, past the Fish Shop.

Fruit and Vegetable Shop. J. Smith.

*Sniff* went Jackie.
*Sniff-sniff* went Phil.

The Fish Shop smelt of apples and
oranges and tomatoes and grapes.
"Oh NO!" said Somebody.
Phil and Jackie looked around,
but there was nobody to be seen.

"In you go!" said Mum. "See you this afternoon!" She pushed Phil and Jackie through the school gates, and swerved off down the pavement doing fifty miles an hour with the pushchair.

Little Acorn School

"Everything smells wrong this morning!" said Phil, when they got inside the school. "Like this corridor."

*Sniff* went Jackie.

*Sniff-sniff* went Phil.

"It ought to smell of polish and chalk," said Phil. "But it doesn't! It smells like ..."

"... like the swimming-pool!" said Jackie.

They both held their noses, and carried on down to Miss Boot's classroom.

Behind them in the corridor, Somebody said: "Oh! No! O-O-H!"

But nobody heard. Everybody was too busy sniffing and getting confused.

Mr Swift's bicycle smelt of roses and
Miss Boot's roses smelt of bicycle
oil. Miss Boot had put on her new
perfume because she was in love
with Mr Swift. She wanted him to
think she smelt lovely.

"What's that awful cabbage smell,
Miss Boot?" Mr Swift said when he
met her in the corridor. "Is it our
school dinner?"

And poor Miss Boot cried.

"Oh, OOH!" said Somebody.

Things got worse by breaktime.
The teachers' *coffee* smelt of *tea*,
and their *tea* smelt of *coffee*, so
nobody drank any of it.

Down the corridor, in Miss Boot's room, everything smelt wrong.

Smoky bacon crisps smelt of cornflakes.

Chocolate smelt of carrots.

And the chalk box smelt of dead dragons with dirty socks!

"**OOOOOH! NOOOOO!**" said Somebody. "I'll lose my job!"

"Every time we sniff something that smells wrong, somebody goes 'Oh' or 'Oh no' or says 'I'll lose my job!'," said Jackie.

"It's only me," said the Somebody, sounding very sad.

Jackie and Phil whirled round.
There, sitting on top of the Games
Box, was the Somebody.

"Sorry," he said. "It's all my
fault!"

"Who are you?" said Phil.

"I'm the Chief Inspector of Smells!" said the Somebody. "I fix the smells when they go wrong."

"Do it then!" said Phil and Jackie.

"Can't!" said the Chief Inspector
of Smells. "I've lost my Smelling
List."

"*Spelling* List?" said Phil.

"SMELLING List," said the Chief
Inspector of Smells. "My List of
Smells. The smells round here have
all got muddled up and I can't put
them right without it."

"Where did you lose it?" said Phil.

"Somewhere in this school!" said the Chief Inspector.

"Hunt the Smelling List!" said Jackie.

And Jackie and Phil and the Chief Inspector of Smells dashed about looking for the Smelling List, but they had to stop when the bell went.

They still hadn't found it by lunch-break, and then things got worse.

Nobody wanted to eat mince meat and cabbage with savoury sauce that smelt like Miss Boot's perfume.

"We won't eat that!" all the children cried.

"Quite right, children," said Miss Boot, and she scolded the cook.

"We want our dinners!" shouted
all the children who took dinners,
and they marched around the school
waving banners and flags.

"There's nothing else for it," said Miss Boot. "Clothes pegs on our noses!"

"Miss, Miss!" said Jackie. "We can't do lessons with clothes pegs on our noses!"

"Right, Jackie," said Miss Boot. "I will send for the parents to take you home. We cannot teach with clothes pegs on our noses either."

"No work with pegs on!" cheered all the children.

"Oh yes, there will be!" said Miss
Boot, and she dashed back to the
Staff Room, and came back with an
armful of Spelling Lists.

"One each to everyone in your
class," she told Phil, and she gave
him a pile.

Phil started giving the Spelling
Lists out. They were like this:

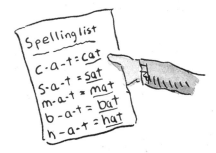

But one wasn't. It was like this:

"Oh!" said Phil, and he stuffed it
up his jumper.

"Now go home with your mums and dads!" said Miss Boot.

They all went home, with pegs on their noses. Most of the mums and dads had pegs on their noses too, because there were odd smells about.

Meanwhile, back at the school, the
Chief Inspector of Smells was hard
at work on the Smelling List Phil
had slipped to him.

Soon, chocolate smelt like chocolate and bacon smelt like bacon and bicycles smelt like bicycles and Miss Boot smelt like lavender, which is sweet. She smelt so sweet that Mr Swift married her, almost at once.

By the next morning, everything
was all right.

Phil and Jackie came down for
breakfast as usual.

"Toast!" said Mum, putting it
down on the table.

*Sniff* went Jackie.

*Sniff-sniff* went Phil.

And they ate it all up, and had
two rounds more, because it smelt so
fresh, and buttery, and lovely!